Dragon in the School

Adapted by Mary Tillworth

Based on the teleplay "Dragon in the School" by Chris Gifford

Illustrated by Dan Haskett and Brenda Goddard

A GOLDEN BOOK • NEW YORK

© 2015 Viacom International Inc. All rights reserved. Published in the United States by Golden Books, an imprint of Random House Children's Books, a division of Penguin Random House LLC, 1745 Broadway, New York, NY 10019, and in Canada by Random House of Canada, a division of Penguin Random House Ltd., Toronto. Golden Books, A Golden Book, A Little Golden Book, the G colophon, and the distinctive gold spine are registered trademarks of Penguin Random House LLC. Nickelodeon, Dora and Friends, and all related titles, logos, and characters are trademarks of Viacom International Inc.
T#: 408452
randomhousekids.com
ISBN 978-0-553-52089-7
Printed in the United States of America
10 9 8 7 6 5 4 3 2

One afternoon outside their school,
Dora and Naiya noticed Pablo heading inside.

"You're not searching for that ancient pool
again, are you?" Dora asked.

"I have to find out if the stories are true,"
Pablo said.

Naiya and Dora joined Pablo. They came upon a secret passageway that led to a dead end.

"*¡Sigue buscando!*" said Dora. "Keep looking! You never know what you might find."

The friends discovered a secret door. "*¡Ábrete, puerta!*" they called—and the door opened!

The friends went down a set of stairs . . .
and found the ancient pool!

As Pablo jumped in, Dora and Naiya studied
a mural on the wall. It told the story of a girl
and a dragon. . . .

The girl and the dragon lived on a beautiful island. Other dragons came to make the island their home, too!

One day, a wizard appeared. He wanted the dragons for himself, so he cast a spell and took all the dragons away.

The girl left the island and went to Dora's school in Playa Verde.

Shortly after, the wizard arrived with his dragons. He wanted to take over the school!

But the big dragon recognized the girl and chased the wizard away!

"I wonder whatever happened to that big dragon?" said Pablo. Just then, bubbles appeared around him. Something was coming up from the bottom!

It was the big dragon!

"Let's get out of here!" cried Pablo.

But Dora ran over to the dragon. She put her hands on her heart. "The dragon needs to know we're friends. *¡Somos amigos!*"

The dragon placed her claws
gently on her heart. She understood
that Dora, Pablo, and Naiya were friends.
   "I think she's protecting something," said
Dora. Suddenly, tiny bubbles appeared on the
water as a baby dragon rose from the pool.

While the baby dragon joined his
mama, they all heard a huge crash.
The mean wizard had returned!
"I want my dragon back!" he cried.

"Go to your home!" Dora told Mama Dragon, pointing to the island on the mural. Mama Dragon gave her baby to Dora to protect. Then she flew up through the ceiling. When the wizard took off after her, Dora and her friends escaped with the baby dragon.

All of Dora's friends wanted to help
return the baby dragon to his mama.
They found a map that led to the
dragon's island home. They boarded a
ship, hoisted the sails, and set off.

As they sailed through the water,
Emma and Pablo spotted the wizard.
He was heading to the island, too!

The friends sped to the island and
landed on a sandy beach. Then they saw
the wizard flying toward them!

"We've got to find somewhere to hide!"
exclaimed Dora.

The friends found a cave and ran inside.

In the darkness, the baby dragon
began to call for his mama.
   "Eee-ee-eeee!" he squeaked. His cries
loosened the cave walls!
   "Rockslide!" yelled Pablo.
   The friends were trapped!

Everyone started to dig—except Pablo.
"Guys, I think Mama Dragon is here in
the cave with us," he whispered.

"Something's glowing up ahead!"
called Pablo.

Dora shined a light—right onto Mama
Dragon! She was having trouble getting
up. Her wing was hurt!

Naiya examined the wing. "I'll need an aloe plant and volcano mud to heal her."

The baby dragon wanted to help. He rushed to the blocked cave entrance and roared so loudly that he cleared away the rocks!

Working together, the friends collected the aloe plant and volcano mud. Alana took them inside and gave them to Naiya. The others were about to follow when the wizard flew down.

"A little dragon! I've always wanted one!" The wizard raised his hands to cast a spell.

Mama Dragon burst from the cave with a roar. Naiya had fixed her wing!

The wizard summoned his other dragons to face Mama Dragon.

"We need help," said Dora. She held out her magic charm bracelet, which had a unicorn charm on it. *"¡Unicornio mágico!"*

When the wizard's dragons
saw the unicorn, they stopped
their attack. Long ago, dragons
and unicorns had made a truce.

Then the dragons roared and broke the wizard's wand so he couldn't cast a spell again.

The defeated wizard hung his head. "I've always wanted to be friends with the dragons," he said softly.

Dora nodded. "You have to ask them."

The wizard put his hands to his heart. *"¿Somos amigos?"* he asked.

Mama Dragon nodded happily.

"We saved the dragons!" cried the friends. *"¡Todos juntos!"*